3

"Look at this boot,"
said Pirate Bill.
"It is not gold."

Pirate Bill

by **Katie Woolley** and **Marcus Cutler**

Pirate Bill had a map.

"Where is the gold?" he said.

"I will dig here."

He looked at the map.

"I will dig here," he said.

"This key is not gold,"
said Pirate Bill.

"Where is the gold?"

Pirate Bill looked at the map.

"I will dig here," he said.

"Oh no!"
said Pirate Bill.
"A shell.
This shell is not gold."

Pirate Bill looked at the map.

"I will dig here," he said.

"Where is the gold?"
shouted Pirate Bill.

He shouted and shouted
and shouted.

"Here is the gold!"
said Pirate Bill.

Story trail

Start at the beginning of the story trail. Ask your child to retell the story in their own words, pointing to each picture in turn to recall the sequence of events.

Start

Independent Reading

This series is designed to provide an opportunity for your child to read on their own. These notes are written for you to help your child choose a book and to read it independently.

In school, your child's teacher will often be using reading books which have been banded to support the process of learning to read.

Use the book band colour your child is reading in school to help you make a good choice. *Pirate Bill* is a good choice for children reading at Yellow Band in their classroom to read independently.

The aim of independent reading is to read this book with ease, so that your child enjoys the story and relates it to their own experiences.

About the book

Pirate Bill has a map and he really wants to dig up the gold. He tries digging all over the park, but the gold is not where he expected it to be!

Before reading

Help your child to learn how to make good choices by asking: "Why did you choose this book? Why do you think you will enjoy it?" Look at the cover together and ask: "What do you think the story will be about?" Support your child to think of what they already know about the story context. Read the title aloud and ask: "What do you think Pirate Bill might be looking for? Why do you think that?" Remind your child that they can try to sound out the letters to make a word if they get stuck.

Decide together whether your child will read the story independently or read it aloud to you. When books are short, as at Yellow Band, your child may wish to do both!

During reading

If reading aloud, support your child if they hesitate or ask for help by telling the word. Remind your child of what they know and what they can do independently.

If reading to themselves, remind your child that they can come and ask for your help if stuck.

After reading

Support comprehension by asking your child to tell you about the story. Use the story trail to encourage your child to retell the story in the right sequence, in their own words.

Help your child think about the messages in the book that go beyond the story and ask: "Do you think Pirate Bill expected the gold to be up in the tree? Why / why not?" Give your child a chance to respond to the story: "Did you have a favourite part? Would you like to find treasure? Have you ever taken part in a treasure hunt?"

Extending learning

Help your child understand the story structure by using the same sentence patterns and adding some new elements. "Let's make up a new story about Pirate Bill looking for gold somewhere else. 'Where is the gold?' said Pirate Bill. 'I will look here,' he said. 'Look at this bag! This bag is not gold!' Now you try. What will Pirate Bill find instead of gold in your story?"

Your child's teacher will be talking about punctuation at Yellow Band. On a few of the pages, check your child can recognise capital letters, question marks, exclamation marks and full stops by asking them to point these out.

Franklin Watts
First published in Great Britain in 2019
by The Watts Publishing Group

Copyright © The Watts Publishing Group 2019

Series Editors: Jackie Hamley and Melanie Palmer
Series Advisors: Dr Sue Bodman and Glen Franklin
Series Designer: Peter Scoulding

A CIP catalogue record for this book is
available from the British Library.

ISBN 978 1 4451 6780 0 (hbk)
ISBN 978 1 4451 6782 4 (pbk)
ISBN 978 1 4451 6781 7 (library ebook)

Printed in China

Franklin Watts
An imprint of
Hachette Children's Group
Part of The Watts Publishing Group
Carmelite House
50 Victoria Embankment
London EC4Y 0DZ

An Hachette UK Company
www.hachette.co.uk

www.franklinwatts.co.uk

FSC
www.fsc.org
MIX
Paper from
responsible sources
FSC® C104740